Dear
Sophia,

I hope you so much
enjoy this book so much
that you will someit
and read it to your own litt-
give someday!

Mimi loves You
So Much

Christmas
2012

This book belongs to

_____

9   8
Digit on the right indicates the number of this printing

Library of Congress Cataloging-in-Publication Number 2001087016

ISBN 978-0–7624–1120–7

Designed by Corinda Cook
Edited by Susan K. Hom
Typography: Caslon and Shelley Allegro

Published by Running Press Classics
an imprint of Running Press Book Publishers
2300 Chestnut Street
Philadelphia, PA 19103-4371

Visit us on the web!
www.runningpress.com

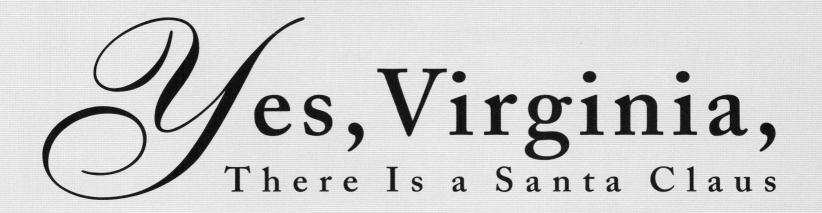

Yes, Virginia,
There Is a Santa Claus

by Francis P. Church
Illustrated by Joel Spector

RP|CLASSICS
PHILADELPHIA · LONDON

In 1897, a young girl wrote to the *New York Sun* asking whether Santa Claus truly existed.

Dear Editor:

I am eight years old.

Some of my little friends say there is no Santa Claus. Papa says if you see it in The Sun it's so.

Please tell me the truth; is there a Santa Claus?

Virginia O'Hanlon.

The paper's response, written by Francis P. Church, appeared in *The Sun* on Sept. 21, 1897.

The Sun

September 21, 1897

Is There a Santa Claus?

We take pleasure in answering at once and thus prominently the communication below, expressing at the same time our great gratification that its faithful author is numbered among the friends of *The Sun*:

Virginia, your little friends are wrong. They have been affected by the skepticism of a skeptical age. They do not believe except what they see. They think that nothing can be which is not comprehensible by their little minds.

*A*ll minds, Virginia, whether they be men's or children's, are little. In this great universe of ours man is a mere insect, an ant, in his

intellect, as compared with the boundless world about him, as measured by the intelligence capable of grasping the whole of truth and knowledge.

Yes, Virginia, there is a Santa Claus. He exists as certainly as love and generosity and devotion exist, and you know that they abound and give to our life its highest beauty and joy.

Alas! how dreary would be the world if there were no Santa Claus. It would be as dreary as if there were no Virginias.

There would be no childlike faith then, no poetry, no romance, to make tolerable this existence. We should have no enjoyment, except in sense and sight. The eternal light with which childhood fills the world would be extinguished.

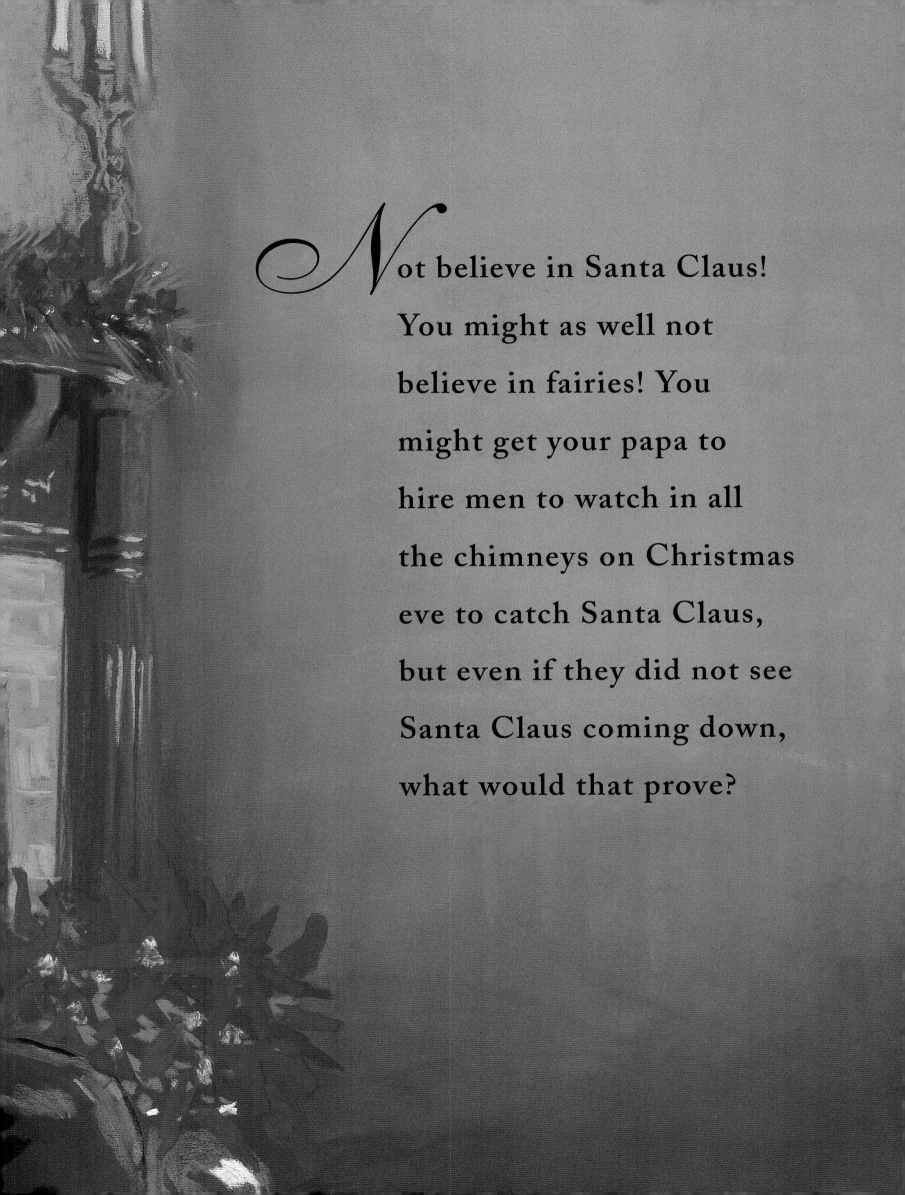

Not believe in Santa Claus! You might as well not believe in fairies! You might get your papa to hire men to watch in all the chimneys on Christmas eve to catch Santa Claus, but even if they did not see Santa Claus coming down, what would that prove?

Nobody sees Santa Claus,
but that is no sign
that there is no Santa Claus.

The most real things in the world are those that neither children nor men can see. Did you ever see fairies dancing on the lawn? Of course not, but that's no proof that they are not there. Nobody can conceive or imagine all the wonders there are unseen and unseeable in the world.

You may tear apart the baby's rattle and see what makes the noise inside but there is a veil covering the unseen world which not the strongest man, nor even the united strength of all the strongest men that ever lived, could tear apart. Only faith, fancy, poetry, love, romance, can push aside that curtain and view and picture the supernal beauty and glory beyond. Is it all real? Ah, Virginia, in all this world there is nothing else real and abiding.

No Santa Claus! Thank God he lives, and he lives forever. A thousand years from now, Virginia, nay, ten times ten thousand years from now, he will continue to make glad the heart of childhood.